So at last he was free
to go home on his own,
Hairy Maclary
with ALL of his bone.

but not Schnitzel von Krumm.

They came to a wall
by the house of Miss Plum.
One of them jumped —

except Bitzer Maloney.

They came to a building site,
cluttered and stony.
Over they went —

except Bottomley Potts.

They came to a yard
full of dinghies and yachts.
Round they all went —

except Muffin McLay.

They came to a hedge
along Waterloo Way.
Under they went —

except Hercules Morse.

They came to the sign
selling Sutherland's Sauce.
Through they all went —

Hungrily sniffing
and licking their chops,
they followed him up
past the school and the shops.

And chasing him home,
with their eyes on the bone,
went Hercules Morse,
Bottomley Potts,
Muffin McLay,
Bitzer Maloney
and Schnitzel von Krumm
with the very low tum.

Then off up the street
on scurrying feet,
on his way to the dairy
went Hairy Maclary.

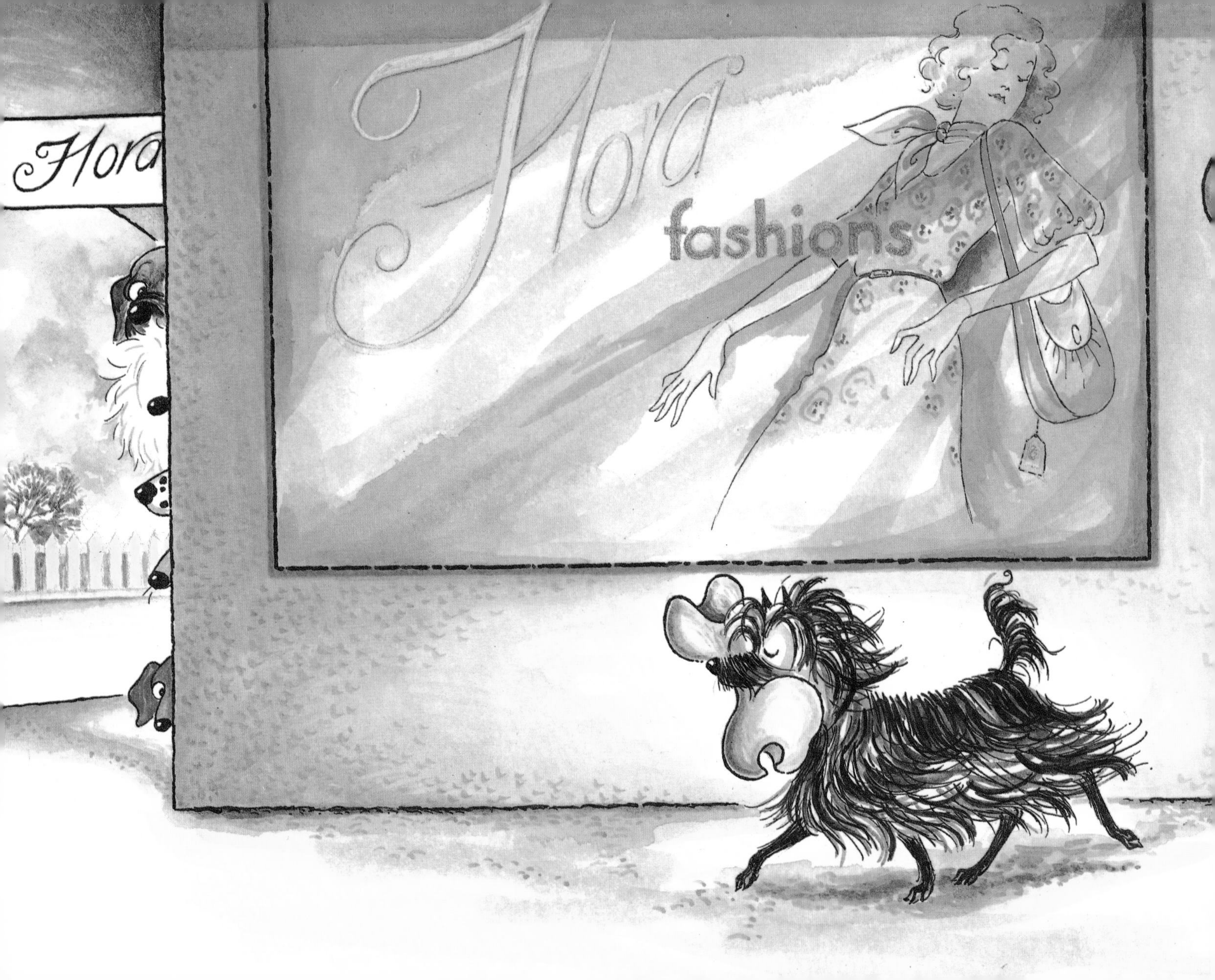
Flora
Flora
fashions

Out of the door
came Samuel Stone.
He gave Hairy Maclary
his tastiest
bone.

Down in the town
by the butcher's shop door,
sat Hairy Maclary
from Donaldson's Dairy.

Hairy Maclary's Bone

Lynley Dodd

GARETH STEVENS

By Lynley Dodd:

The Nickle Nackle Tree
My Cat Likes to Hide in Boxes (with Eve Sutton)

GOLD STAR FIRST READERS
Hairy Maclary from Donaldson's Dairy   The Apple Tree
Hairy Maclary's Bone   The Smallest Turtle
Hairy Maclary Scattercat   Wake Up, Bear

Library of Congress Cataloging in Publication Data

Dodd, Lynley.
  Hairy Maclary's bone.

  Summary: A small black dog uses a slick
maneuver to protect his bone from his canine friends.
  [1. Dogs — Fiction. 2. Stories in rhyme] I. Title.
PZ8.3.D637Hal   1985   [E]   85-9772
ISBN 0-918831-26-1
ISBN 0-918831-06-7 (lib. bdg.)

North American edition first published in 1985 by
Gareth Stevens, Inc.
7317 West Green Tree Road
Milwaukee, Wisconsin 53223, USA

First published by
Mallinson Rendel Publishers Ltd.

©Lynley Dodd, 1984

Typography by Sharon Burris.

Hairy Maclary's
Bone